For my darling kai

First published 2002 by Macmillan Children's Books
This edition published 2003 by Macmillan Children's Books
a division of Macmillan Publishers Limited
20 New Wharf Road, London N1 9RR
Basingstoke and Oxford
Associated companies throughout the world
www.panmacmillan.com

ISBN-13: 978-0-333-96622-8
ISBN-10: 0-333-96622-8

Text and Illustration copyright © Jane Cabrera 2002
Moral rights asserted.

7 9 8

A CIP catalogue record for this book is available
from the British Library.

Printed in China

The Polar Bear and the Snow Cloud

by Jane Cabrera

The Polar Bear and the Snow Cloud

by Jane Cabrera

MACMILLAN CHILDREN'S BOOKS

There was once a polar bear whose only friend was a fluffy white snow cloud.

He loved the cloud,
but he wished for a friend
he could play with.

The snow cloud felt sorry for
the polar bear, so he decided to
make him a friend.
  Very carefully, he dropped
snowflakes down into the
shape of an owl.

The polar bear was very happy.
  "Maybe he will play with me,"
he thought.

So the polar bear threw a snowball
at the owl. It landed with a soft
squelch on its head. But the owl did
not move or hoot because it was
only made of snow.

The next day it had melted away.

The snow cloud tried again.
This time he made a big whale.
"Maybe we can swim and splash
together," thought the polar bear.

So the polar bear jumped into the water and swam towards the whale. But it just floated away without a sound. The next day the whale had melted away.

The snow cloud tried again. This time
he made a seal. The polar bear took
her a fish as a present.
"Maybe she will be my friend,"
he thought.

But snow seals don't eat fish,
so the polar bear sadly took the
fish away and ate it on his own.
The next day, the snow seal
had melted away.

The snow cloud tried one last time.
He dropped snowflakes slowly down
into the shape of a reindeer.

  "Perhaps she will play hide-and-seek
with me," the polar bear wondered,
and off he went to hide.

The polar bear hid for a long time.
But the reindeer never moved.
The polar bear knew that, like
all his other snow friends, the
reindeer would just melt away.

He was just about to walk away
when a snowflake drifted slowly
down onto the new polar bear's nose.
And the new polar bear . . .

let out an enormous
sneeze . . .

ACHOO!

"You're real!" gasped the polar bear.
"Will you play with me?"
And he did. They played tag and
hide-and-seek, and the snow cloud
dropped snowflakes for them to chase.
And the polar bear was very,
very happy.